DATE DUE

For ALexis and WiLLeM
and in Loving memory of BiLL Morgan

I would like to thank Esther Shipman for reminding me that the environmental
nursery rhymes I had written in the 1980s were, unfortunately, still relevant
and for suggesting that I reissue them. My thanks also to Doris Anderson, who from
early on encouraged me to speak out – with words or pictures.
And thanks to designer Michael Solomon. BK

Groundwood Books / House of Anansi Press
110 Spadina Avenue, Suite 801, Toronto, Ontario M5V 2K4
Distributed in the USA by Publishers Group West
1700 Fourth Street, Berkeley, CA 94710

ONTARIO ARTS COUNCIL
CONSEIL DES ARTS DE L'ONTARIO

We acknowledge for their financial support of our publishing program the Canada Council for the Arts, the Government
of Canada through the Book Publishing Industry Development Program (BPIDP) and the Ontario Arts Council.

Library and Archives Canada Cataloguing in Publication
Klunder, Barbara
Other goose: recycled rhymes for our fragile times / written and illustrated by Barbara Wyn Klunder.
Includes index.
ISBN-13: 978-0-88899-829-3
ISBN-10: 0-88899-829-5
1. Environmental degradation–Juvenile poetry. 2. Environmental protection–Juvenile poetry.
3. Children's poetry, Canadian (English). I. Title.
PS8621.L85O84 2007   jC811'.6   C2007-901156-X

The illustrations were done in pen and ink. Printed on Reincarnation Matte paper, which is 100% recycled with 50%
post-consumer waste and is processed chlorine-free. The decorative font in this book is KlunderScript, designed by
Barbara Wyn Klunder and available from Font Shop, Berlin. Book design by Michael Solomon.
Printed and bound in Canada.

OtHer Goose

Recycled Rhymes for Our Fragile Times...

Written & illustrated by

BarbaraWyn Klunder

GROUNDWOOD BOOKS
HOUSE OF ANANSI PRESS
TORONTO   BERKELEY

LittLe Miss Muffet

Little Miss Muffet
Had quite enough of it –
Clouds of second-hand smoke.

Along came a spider
Who was also a writer
And together they tried not to choke!

Rock-a-Bye Baby

Rock-a-bye baby
On a tree top.
All of this logging
Has got to stop.

'Cause trees breathe in
What we breathe out.
That's what Nature
Is all about.

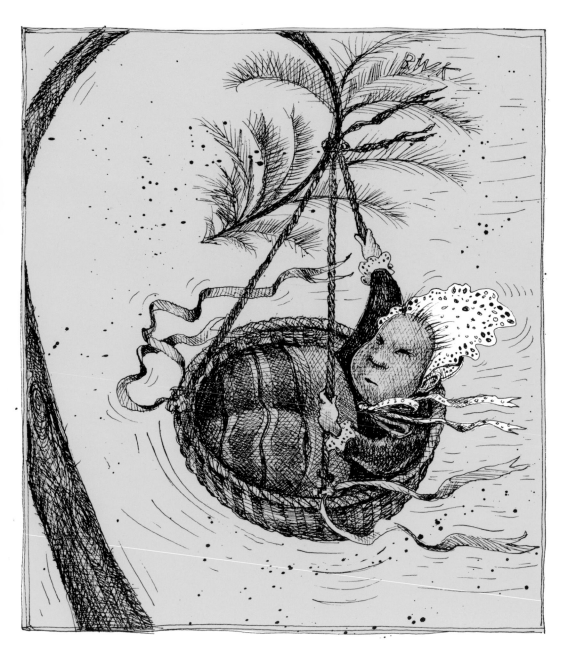

This Little Piggy

This little piggy
Went to market.
Couldn't find a place
To park it.
So he sold it.

Little Bo-Peep

Little Bo-Peep
Is one of the sheep
Found at the shopping center.
Leave her alone
And she's liable to clone.
But isn't that why you sent her?

{ 11 }

LittLe Boy BLue

Little Boy Blue
Come blow your horn!
What goes into the ground
Comes out in the corn.

Old Mother Hubbard

Old Mother Hubbard
Went to the cupboard
To get her poor dog a bone.

When she got there
The cupboard was bare...
So the food bank gave her a loan.

Humpty Dumpty

Humpty Dumpty
Had a great lake.
Humpty Dumpty
Made a mistake.
All the king's chemicals,
All the king's waste
Went into the lake,
For goodness' sake!

There Was an OLd WoMan

There was an old woman
Who lived in a shoe.
She had so many kids
But – knew what to do –
She started a band.

Jack and Jill

Jack and Jill went up the hill
To fetch a glass of water.
After a drink
They started to think
Of all the germs
And microworms –
It's a form of urban slaughter!
So Jill bought her water.

Hey, Diddle Diddle

Hey, diddle diddle,
The cat played the fiddle and
The cow recorded the tune.
The laughing dog
Sent out his blog
And the dish sailed right past the moon.

Mary, Mary, Quite Contrary

Mary, Mary, quite contrary,
How does your garden grow?
With weeding and watering,
Selling and bartering,
It's amazing how dung turns to dough!

OLd KiNG CoLe

Old King Cole
Was a merry old soul,
And a very cool soul was he.
Jazz, hip-hop or singing the blues –
He jammed 'til a quarter to three.

Sing a Song of Sixth Sense

Sing a song of sixth sense,
A pocket full of lies.
Big business runs the headlines.
Do you really think that's wise?

If a politician says it's white,
You know for sure it's black.
And then they beg for all of us
To vote them safely back.

Hickory, Dickory, Dock

Hickory, dickory, dock
We're always racing the clock.
The clock strikes one,
The meltdown's begun.
And on we run,
Hickory, dickory, dock.

Mary Had a Little Lamb

Mary had a little lamb,
Henry had the fish.
But everywhere that Mary went
He tasted half her dish.

He followed her to lunch one day
And thought that she would buy it.
"I think it's time you paid," she said.
"And time for you to diet."

{ 33 }

Baa, Baa, Black Sheep

Baa, baa, black sheep,
Have you any gas?
Are you kidding me, man?
No one has!

Gas for the delivery trucks,
Gas for the jet planes,
Gas for all those giant cars
Parked down the lane.

BLow, BLow, BLow Your Nose

Blow, blow, blow your nose
And watch out where you sneeze!
Grass and weeds,
Nuts and seeds
All seem to make you wheeze.

There Was a Crooked Man

There was a crooked man
Who walked a crooked mile.
Whenever he could rip you off
He smiled a crooked smile.

He owned a crooked dealership
And tricked whoever bought.
He gained a crooked leadership
And never did get caught.

The Queen of Tarts

The Knave of Art
Stole her heart
With the work he did.
The Queen of Tarts
Was charmed for starts
So for his work she bid.
    Art does take money and does take time.
    But craft without concept ain't worth a dime.

Jack Be Nimble

Jack be nimble
Jack be quick
Jack watch out
For that oil slick!

Twinkle, Twinkle, Little Starlets

Twinkle, twinkle, little starlets
More and more resembling harlots
Up above the world so high –
Celebrity fame's the reason why.

Star Light, Star Bright

Star light, star bright
First star I see tonight.
I wish the air
Was nice and clear
So I could see you every night.

Index

Little Miss Muffet 4

Rock-a-Bye Baby 6

This Little Piggy 8

Little Bo-Peep 10

Little Boy Blue 12

Old Mother Hubbard 14

Humpty Dumpty 16

There Was an Old Woman 18

Jack and Jill 20

Hey, Diddle Diddle 22

Mary, Mary, Quite Contrary 24

Old King Cole 26

Sing a Song of Sixth Sense 28

Hickory, Dickory, Dock 30

Mary Had a Little Lamb 32

Baa, Baa, Black Sheep 34

Blow, Blow, Blow Your Nose 36

There Was a Crooked Man 38

The Queen of Tarts 40

Jack Be Nimble 42

Twinkle, Twinkle, Little Starlets 44

Star Light, Star Bright 46